THE ALIEN'S PAST

GRACE KENSINGTON

1

———

For the second time Ivy had walked through the compound and to the boundary that kept it separated from the rest of the planet. She felt like she was repeating the same steps as she had, wondering if her feet were falling into the same places that they had when she made her first journey toward the settlement. When she looked down at the ground in front of her it was as if she could see the hint of the outlines of footprints still marking the rich, dark dirt where they had not yet been able to resolve themselves through time or rain. She wished that she could tell which of those steps belonged to her and which belonged to Maxim. Had she been able to, she would have taken the time to rest her feet into his prints, finding comfort in the guidance that they would offer. It was as though if she followed along in her own footsteps she would be making the same journey, heading into the unknown with the same sense of insecurity and hint of fear that was there when she made this journey for the first time. If she chose Maxim's steps, however, though they were facing in the direction of the compound rather than toward the settlement, she wouldn't be blind, she would know where she was going and his presence still in those steps would protect her.

When the wall was finally at their back and they were walking across the wide, open section of the planet, Ivy had a strange feeling that she hadn't had before. The thoughts that she had the first time that she left the compound and headed toward the settlement with the women and George repeated themselves through her mind, but there were like they were coming through water at her. Images and questions that she asked herself swam through a haze, occasionally coming close enough to her consciousness that she could examine them and explore them again in the context of what she had experienced and now knew.

At the beginning of her first journey toward the settlement her mind had felt out of control. Everything had happened so quickly from the moment that she arrived until they packed up and left to go help the men as they struggled to figure out what to do about the people who had been locked in place by the Covra that Ivy didn't even feel like she knew what he was supposed to be thinking or how she should handle it. She struggled to bring her mind into the present moment, to force herself to realize that everything that was happening really was. No longer was her visit to Uoria about being a part of a scientific expedition or helping George participate in the exchange program between the university and the Denynso. No longer was she going to be spending a few months at the compound doing research that she had been dreaming about doing throughout her entire education and compiling reports that would make her the pride and the envy of the science community.

Instead, she had been thrust into an exhilarating but frightening project that had them dealing with plants that she had never heard of and concepts that were so far out of her mind that she would never have believed them even possible much less something that she would actually be dealing with in her time on Uoria. She had done everything that she could to help throughout their long days and nights trying to find the resolution that the men so desperately needed. She had given every bit of input that she could and pushed herself to her absolute limits trying to come up with new thoughts and new angles that they could take to find the right help. They told her that she had been helpful and reassured her that they were glad that she had come, but Ivy knew deep within her that she was never completely convinced that they were telling her the truth. Even as they were all standing together leaning over the table in the healer's office going through the pages of his old books and examining the supplies and materials that he had left behind, she found herself wondering how much of the acceptance that they showed her was actually for her, and how much of it was because they had come to accept George and he had stood beside her to act as her advocate and representative during the struggle with Creia that happened as soon as her shuttle arrived.

The worst of the feelings of uncertainty that she had gone through during those early days had come from the way that the Denynso woman Zsilvia looked at her. Ivy didn't know anything about her, and hadn't even spoken a single word to her, and yet the woman glared at her with a level of hatred and distrust that she couldn't understand. Of course, now she knew that Zsilvia had felt that way about her because of her deep love for George and her misconception that Ivy and George were somehow involved in a relationship that went beyond their professional link. Though she was extremely fond of George and considered him one of the most impressive and amazing men who she had ever met, there had never been anything in their relationship beyond the work that they did together and the closeness that formed in that context. When she finally realized what was happening she approached Zsilvia to explain what their relationship really was, and now she and George had become mates in the tradition of her kind, but there was still the lingering feeling of her eyes burrowing into her, questioning her, wondering if her motivations for being on the planet were really what she said they were. Even though the Denynso woman didn't look at her that way any longer, Ivy still struggled with feeling like she was somehow less than them, not quite fitting in enough to be a part of the group that was forming, and yet also a small piece that would make it so that the group wasn't ever the same again should she not be there.

That first trip she had been taken completely off-guard by how quickly and profoundly her visions of her time on Uoria had changed. She had been thinking about the settlement that she had only just found out existed, and what was going to happen when they arrived, trying to force her mind to focus in like the people around her seemed to be doing. Ivy glanced beside her as she thought about this and saw Maxim walking along beside her, the look on his face serious as he seemed drawn into the horizon ahead of them. She realized as she looked at him that in thinking about her first journey toward the settlement it hadn't occurred to her that when she took those steps, she didn't yet know Maxim. The imprints that her feet had left in the dirt leading through the settlement the first time where intrinsically different from those that now layered atop the ones returning because they were made by steps infinitely more unsure of themselves, wandering along a path that she didn't know and had yet to begin to understand. Now, though, her steps were more solid because they moved alongside Maxim's, more confident because they fell into the prints that he made, and more secure because she knew that from now on, no matter where those footprints led, they would never mark the earth alone.

This thought settled her mind and helped it to feel more in control as they continued forward toward the sky that had taken on a deep pink color and was now streaked with the foggy purple clouds of impending night. Rather than feeling like she was walking into the unknown and wondering what she was going to encounter next, the surroundings were familiar. There was even the sense as she looked at Rain, Lynx, and the others who had joined them in returning to the settlement that she, in a way, was even more prepared for this journey than they were. They had only traveled from the compound to the settlement and back again. Ivy and Maxim had escaped the settlement and journeyed all the way to his kingdom and then through the areas of the planet that even the Denysno had not yet seen.

The sudden thought of Maxim's kingdom made the breath catch in her throat. She thought about what he had said to her when they were talking about the fact that he wanted to return to the settlement rather than immediately going to Earth like many of the others. She knew he didn't just intend to go to the settlement and free the other Mikana. He wanted to return to his kingdom and unravel the mysteries surrounding the Order and the death of his father. She could see it in the way he carried himself, in the way that he watched the planet as it unfolded in front of him. He was holding a deep sense of responsibility and duty in his heart, but those compulsions were balanced by feelings of distrust and wariness that made him want to go beyond what he was told to what really existed in those tunnels and behind the hidden doors that his kind walked over every day, yet didn't know they were there.

2

————

"Can you tell me more about the Order?" Ivy asked.

The light was nearly gone and they had finally settled down for the night, knowing that they wouldn't be able to get any further without having to use their light sticks to illuminate their way. Though this was a possibility, Rain and Rey had felt uneasy about the prospect of venturing through the darkness not knowing what could be lurking around them, watching them by the glow of their own lights. They had stopped close to the site where they had rested on their other journeys and created their camp for the night, the group dividing so that the two couples broke away from the rest to set up their tents.

Maxim was spreading a thick blanket on the ground to provide cushioning and warmth as they slept, but when he heard her question he sat back on his feet and looked around his shoulder at her.

"Why do you want to know?" he asked.

She heard the hesitation in his voice, but she needed to know, so she pressed forward, reaching into one of her bags to withdraw a pair of lighter clothing to wear to sleep so that she didn't have to continue looking at him as she spoke.

"It's important to you," she said. "I stayed here rather than going back to Earth because it mattered so much to you. I think that, that means I deserve to know as much as I possibly can about what's going on. If I'm going to help you, I need to understand."

"You're going to help me?" he asked.

"Of course," she said, sitting down so that she could start to undress. "If I didn't want to help you, I wouldn't be here. I would have gone back to Earth and just hoped that someday you would be able to join me. Instead, I stayed. You told me how important it was to you to tell your brother what you've found out and to find out more about your father and the Order. I just want to know what you know so that I can do everything I can to help you. I don't want this hanging over us for the rest of our lives. I want you to find out whatever it is that you need to know that will put your mind at ease and give you peace so that we can really start our life together."

She lifted her eyes to Maxim and saw him staring down at the blanket, his fingertips tracing along the stitches in the fabric absently.

"I remember the night my father died."

Ivy felt her heart clench. She hated hearing the heaviness in his voice that seemed to come from deep inside of him.

"You do?" she asked, not really knowing what else to say.

Maxim looked up at her and nodded slightly.

"At least, I remember the night that we found out that he was dead. I don't really know when he died."

"Who told you that he had died?" Ivy asked carefully.

"Athan."

"The old man at the gate in the kingdom? The one who showed us the tunnels?"

Maxim nodded again.

"He's known my family since long before I was born. He was the one who came to our house that night and told us that my father hadn't survived the mission that they had gone on."

"What mission?" Ivy asked.

She dropped her nightshirt over her head and lay on her side so that she was closer to him, somehow offering him protection and comfort with the curve of her body around him.

"They were doing something for the Order. They had left almost a month before and when Athan returned he looked battered and starved. He wouldn't tell us where they had been or what they had been doing. All he said was that my father was dead."

"Where is he buried?"

Maxim's eyes grew cold and dark. He shook his head, looking away from her and focusing again on the stitches of the blanket beneath him.

"We never got to bury him," he said, his voice suddenly hoarse with emotion.

"What happened?" she asked.

"We never got his body back."

For a moment Ivy regretted asking the question. She didn't want to cause Maxim any more pain than he had already had to go through in the last few weeks, especially when it came to his father. She couldn't imagine what it would be like to lose her father in such a way. Though they didn't see each other as often as she would have liked once she started working with George, she knew that he was there, that he was just a phone call away and that if at any moment she needed him, her father would have gotten to her as quickly as he could to help her with anything that was within his ability to do. The thought of him simply being gone, killed in some unknown place and not even returned so that her family could bury him properly was excruciating.

She knew, though, that this was not the only pain of Maxim's that she would experience, or the only time that he would have to confront his memories of his father's death. If he really was dedicated to peeling back all of these layers and discovering the truth, there were going to be many more moments when she would feel the pain coming off of him and hear the regret in his voice. It was excruciating, but she had to believe that in each moment of that pain he was getting stronger, and together they were getting closer to the life that she wanted so desperately for them.

"Do you know what happened to it?" she asked, reaching out to rest her hand on his leg comfortingly.

"No."

"Athan didn't tell you?"

Maxim sighed and shook his head again. There was a flicker of emotion across his face that was close to anger, but it was fleeting and when he spoke she didn't hear it in his voice.

"He was only allowed to tell us that my father died, nothing else. Remember, we aren't even supposed to know that the Order exists. Even though we are from the original line, we weren't supposed to know until we were selected."

"But he helped us in those tunnels."

"It was expected that my brother and I would be selected for the Order. No one knows why or how anyone got selected, or even who is the one that does the selection, but because every other generation of men before us had been in it, my father just assumed that we would be, and he told us what he could to prepare us. Athan has been much the same way. He's told me what he could, but he is still very much under the control of the Order. The consequences of someone finding out that he had even known that we knew and didn't do anything about it could be dire."

Ivy suddenly remembered something that Maxim's mother had said when they were talking to her about the Order and her late husband when they were in the kingdom. She could remember the look in Ellora's eyes when Maxim started talking about the Klimnu and when she revealed that the rest of the Order already knew what had happened to the group that had split off from them, the segment of rogues that the rest of the Mikana had been taught had ventured out onto the planet and died, but who Ivy and the others now knew had actually become the gruesome and detested enemies of the Denynso and all others they encountered.

"Your mother said that your father died because of the Klimnu. What did she mean by that?"

"I don't know. The way she said it sounds like he went against the Order in some way, but if they were forming alliances to fight against the Klimnu, what could he have done to incite them to kill him?"

"Maxim," Ivy said carefully, hesitating saying the words that were weaving through her mind and tormenting the backs of her thoughts, "could your father..."

"Have been one of the Klimnu?" Maxim finished after her voice trailed off. "That thought has been killing me since my mother mentioned that my father was killed because of the Order and what they knew."

"Do you think that it could possibly be true?" she asked.

She couldn't bear the thought that this amazing man,

this beautiful, courageous man who she loved so fully and completely, could have come from one of those horrific creatures, but she also couldn't forget the way his skin dissolved beneath the touch of the flowers and the violent reaction that he'd had to Pyra when they encountered him among the wreckage of the Nyx 23 ship.

"It could be true that they killed my father because they were trying to fight against the Klimnu after they destroyed all of the allies of the Order and threatened the rest of the planet and he was one of those creatures or betrayed the Order and its allies to the Klimnu."

"But?" she asked, hearing the hint of hesitation in his voice that told her that he was thinking something else.

"But what if there's more to it than that? What if it wasn't that he was aligned with the Klimnu and trying to infiltrate the Order as part of their efforts to take over the planet...?"

"But that he wasn't..."

3

———

"Why do you think that they chose us?"

Rain was lying on her back staring at the roof of the tent above her and imagining the stars just beyond it. She could feel Lynx close beside her and the warmth of his body made the darkness of the tent feel comforting and protective rather than frightening. She was glad that they had stopped for the night rather than continuing onward as Ivy and some of the others had suggested. Not only did it mean that they weren't roaming the large, open area of the planet completely vulnerable, but she also felt like she needed as much rest as she could get before they got back to the settlement. What awaited them there was still unknown, and she wanted to be prepared for whatever they might encounter.

"What do you mean?" Lynx asked, sliding over slightly so that his shoulder touched hers and she could feel his hip against her.

"Why do you think that the Valdicians chose us to send here?"

"I thought that they sent you here so that the Covra could use you."

"Was that always the plan, though? The Valdicians didn't know that we were going to the prison planet. They would have had no way of planning that they would send us to Uoria for the use of the Covra, and I don't think this was something that they just came up with during our struggle on the planet. So did they always have the plan of sending some hapless crew to become enslaved by the Covra and help them with their quest to take over Uoria and it just so happened that we were the ones that showed up at the right time to be the ones that they sent, or did they always have a target on Earth humans?"

"A target?"

"Humans are a commodity, they always have been. We're strong, advanced, and plentiful, but seem to have a much stronger concept of justice and humane treatment of other species than others do." She looked over at Lynx. "I'm sorry. I didn't mean to imply..."

"No," he said, "it's alright. You're right. The Denynso are far bigger and stronger, but we are nowhere near as plentiful. We are, however, ruthless and violent when necessary. It's no big secret that the humans are far less likely to fight and more likely to try to save others than the Denynso."

"That is exactly why so many other species have come for us, though," Rain said. "They know that capturing some of us would give them a much better chance of taking over Earth. Could they really have just planned to send any group that happened to be close enough to take over, or did they somehow know that with what they were doing on that planet that eventually a team from Earth would arrive and they could send them to Uoria with the intention that that crew would not only become the slaves of the Covra and the

Valdician allies, but that they would lure others from Earth who would come hoping to find and save them?"

"How, though?" Lynx asked. "You said yourself that the people of Earth didn't even know that Uoria existed when you left. If the Validicians wanted to lure others from Earth, why would they force you to crash on a planet that the people who would be out looking for you wouldn't know was there much less think to look for you on, while also disabling all of your communication technology so that you wouldn't even be able to let others know that you were in trouble and possibly ask for them to come rescue you?"

His words were at once painful and reassuring. She didn't want to think that the mission that she had so carefully helped to plan and execute had actually guided them directly into the path of the Valdicians, but at the same time it was comforting to think that the people of Earth didn't simply not look for them.

"Did you ever think that you would get rescued?" Lynx asked.

His voice was soft, hesitant as he asked the question that seemed just as painful for him as it was for her. She remembered the last time she had heard his voice sounding like that and her stomach felt sick. Then she didn't know what he looked like and had never touched his skin. That was when she was still locked in place and unable to move her body or open her eyes. Lynx didn't know for sure then that she was able to hear him when he spoke to her, yet every time that he was in the room with her he had talked to her, told her what was happening, and reassured her of how hard he was working to try to find a way to release her from the torturous bonds of the Covra.

It was listening to his voice that had brought Rain out of the deep darkness of the lock placed on her, but also kept her just out of his reach. She didn't know then that it was because he was Denynso, a species close enough to human that his voice began to release the lock on her, but not close enough to completely free her. So she continued to listen to him, falling in love with him as she waited patiently, knowing that he was doing everything that he could and believing with everything that she had that he would one day be successful and she would be able to live again. His voice had stayed slightly sad, though, and it hurt her even then to hear that painful hint in each word that he said. It wasn't until she had heard the voice of the woman, a woman she later learned wasn't even in the room with them but communicating with them through a piece of technology that she had never seen and didn't understand, that she had felt her mind release and her body come back into her own control. Finally she was able to open her eyes and see Lynx for the first time and feel his skin beneath her fingertips. Finally his voice didn't sound so sad.

Now, though, the sadness had returned and she knew that he was thinking about the years before he had found her, years before he even came into existence. It was still difficult for her sometimes to wrap her mind around the idea that she had lived the majority of her life before Lynx was even born, yet she had been intended as his mate from the moment of his birth. He knew the instant that he saw her that she was meant to be his, and even finding out that she had been locked in sleep for one hundred years hadn't dissuaded him from knowing that they were meant to spend their lives together. He knew that if she didn't come out of the lock or if she didn't fall in love with him, that he would live his entire life alone and longing for the mate that he never bonded with.

She hated that the sadness had returned to his voice, but

she understood why it was there. As painful as it was for her to think of the time that she had been without him, it was even more difficult for Lynx because he felt that he had failed her. Even though he wasn't even born for most of her life and he had no way of knowing that she existed, he felt that he hadn't lived up to his responsibilities to guard, protect, and nurture her. Part of him felt that he had allowed the lock to happen, had allowed her to languish in the bed that she had simply laid down on to rest and then didn't leave for more than a century. They had talked very little of the time before he had found her. Though she had told Pyra and the others everything that they had wanted to know and helped them to understand the Covra, Lynx hadn't asked her to tell him about what she had gone through. Now it seemed that he was ready to know more and she had to be courageous enough to tell him.

4

Rain took a breath and nodded.

"There was a short time when we first arrived on Uoria that I really believed that we would be rescued. I don't even remember if I told any of the others, but I just had this feeling that they were going to come for us. Of course, this was before we found out about the Covra."

"Why did you leave Earth in the first place?" Lynx asked.

She looked at him strangely, rising up onto her elbow so that she could look at him more closely.

"I told you. I was part of a team that left on a mission to explore beliefs that a species was utilizing a planet as an illegal prison camp."

"I know about Nyx 23," Lynx said. "I know that you had a job, but you never really explained why you did it, or what happened after you left."

"Do you really want to know?"

"Yes."

"When I was on Earth I was part of a small paramilitary operative that focused on illegal and unethical activities by other species and on other planets. We had received intelligence that what was widely accepted as a barren and unexplored planet was actually being used as a prisoner of war colony designed and operated not in compliance with the intergalactic agreements. The information came from a source that wasn't recognized and many people in our faction didn't believe that it was accurate. They thought that it was a conspiracy theory that had no basis in reality."

"How could you not know, though?"

"What do you mean?"

"How could you have not known that that planet was being used that way?"

Rain suddenly felt extremely defensive. She sat up sharply and stared at him.

"You didn't know that there was another species living right beneath your feet for your entire life, or that there was an entire settlement of people locked in place right on the other side of your planet, or that the enemies that you thought you had eliminated actually still existed and was living perfectly contentedly less than a four day's journey away from you. How did you not know any of that?"

"It wasn't my job to know any of that," Lynx said, the defensive tone rising in his voice as well.

"It was your duty, Lynx. As a Denynso warrior, you are bound to protect your planet and your kind, and that means knowing the threats that are there so that you can fight against them."

Lynx looked stung and his jaw hardened.

"You're right," he said. "I failed at my duty, and I will never be able to forgive myself for it."

"You shouldn't have to forgive yourself for anything," Rain told him, the anger starting to melt out of her. "You did everything that you knew to do. It wasn't your fault that you weren't given all of the information that you needed to know what you were up against."

She stopped short of mentioning that the blame actually fell on his king Creia, the powerful monarch of the Denynso clan who purposely avoided telling his people everything that he knew about the risks and threats that lurked on the planet. He hadn't known everything that was going on, on Uoria, but he had known enough that he should have told his people more. He expected that the warriors would devote their lives to protecting the planet and guarding their kind, and yet he hadn't told them everything that he knew about the origins of their kind or the other species that had built the planet as it was today.

"Tell me what happened," Lynx finally said, sounding as though he wanted to distance himself from his own failures and the lingering questions and doubts that kept him feeling somewhat off balance.

"You have to realize that the people of Earth knew far less about the galaxy then, than they do now. There were still many planets and species that we didn't know anything about, and a lot of people were unwilling to take risks to find out more. When we heard about the prison colony, the group that I worked for was divided over what we were going to do. Some didn't want to give it any credence and thought we should just move on. Some even thought that it was a setup and that if we did anything about it, it could lead to a war. The rest of us thought that it was worth the lives of whoever was being held on the planet to find out what was going on. We figured that there were two possible negative outcomes that could happen if we went. We could get to the planet and find that it was, in fact, deserted and that we had wasted the time and resources of the depart-ment. Or we could get there, find out that the information was accurate, and be put into a dangerous situation with the Valdicians."

"Did you know of the Valdicians before then?"

"Vaguely. We had heard of them and knew that they were not exactly the friendliest of species, but until then we hadn't had any contact with them."

"So you just left?"

"Not quite. The group of us who knew that there were dangers that we would likely face if we went on the mission and still knew that it was worth it split off from the rest and formed our own committee within the department so that the others could focus on the other projects that they felt were more promising than this one. Fortunately we had the support of the majority of the heads of the department and they enabled us to spend some more time gathering as much information as we could and prepare for the mission. When we left, we were using some of the most advanced technology available. Our Star City ship was exactly what it sounds like, a little city that could travel through space. It had everything that our group of more than 200 needed to survive the journey. It would take weeks to get to the planet, and that was in a ship that was among the fastest available."

"What happened when you got there?"

"The plan was that we would approach the planet in an orbiting pattern so that we would be more difficult to detect. We would be able to recognize any abnormalities on the surface of the planet that might indicate large buildings as we approached. We would gather as much information as we could, then land and infiltrate. The hope was that we would be able to free the prisoners and capture the Valdicians. If we weren't able to, we would send communication back to mission control and leave. When they arrived with more units, we would all return to the planet to complete the mission."

"When did you realize that something wasn't going the way that you wanted it to?"

"Everything seemed fine as we approached the planet. As we got within the orbit of the planet it didn't take long for us to see that the information about the prison colony was absolutely true. There were dozens of buildings spread across the center of the planet and massive walls surrounding them." Rain stopped, suddenly feeling her lungs closing, making it more difficult to release and draw in breaths. She gathered herself, pushing forward. "As soon as we saw it, we knew that we couldn't wait to collect information before we landed. We found a place as far from the buildings as we could and landed. I will never be able to forget what it was like when we stepped out onto the planet for the first time."

Rain felt her mind travel to that first moment when she left the Star City ship the first time. She could still feel the crunching of the dry, pebbly ground beneath her boots and the searing of the intense, almost oppressive heat on her skin. Her eyes closed and she felt her body sway as the overwhelming memories of the screams washed over her. She could hear the voice's cutting through the still air and seeming to sink down to her bones, trembling across them until she felt sick. She wished that she could forget those screams, that she didn't have to continue to hear them reverberating through her mind and reminding her of everything that she saw when they stormed the prison colony and encountered the Valdicians and the prisoners that they held captive on that horrible planet.

The warmth of Lynx's hand against her cheek brought Rain out of the darkness of her thoughts and she turned her face so that she could touch a kiss to his hand. The scent of his skin and the familiarity of his touch soothed her, quieting the disturbing sounds that ricocheted through her mind and shook deep within her soul. She focused on the sound of his breathing, imagining the air moving through his body and back out into the close space of the tent so that she could breathe it in.

"You don't have to tell me anymore," he said, rubbing the pad of his thumb across her cheekbone. "It's alright."

Rain nodded and brought her hand up to cover his, letting her fingers slip between his so that they intertwined lightly on her cheek. She drew her fingertips down along the back of his hand and along his arm until they reached his shoulder. As she traced his arm with her fingers, Lynx brought his hand down from her cheek so that it trailed along her jawbone and then onto the side of her neck. The touch of his fingers on this tender, vulnerable skin made her shiver and she tilted her head slightly to offer him more access. He took the invitation and continued his slow, careful exploration of her neck, bringing his fingers around to the front so that he could trail the tips into the soft dip between her collarbones.

As Lynx's fingers traveled down the front of her chest toward the swell of her breasts Rain could feel her breath quickening. Her hand had fallen away from his shoulder and she brought both to his lap now, running them along his thighs with the same slow, precise attention that he was giving her skin. She wasn't wearing anything beneath her nightgown and she could feel her taut nipples pressing against the thin fabric as if trying to reach Lynx. He didn't make them wait long. His hands came to the blue satin ribbon at her neckline and pulled on one end, releasing the bow and loosening the crossed pattern along the front. This caused the gown to become slack enough that it slipped from her shoulders and Lynx guided it the rest of the way off so that it pooled around her ribs.

Rain drew her arms out of the gown slowly. Her mate looked at her with such intensity, such hunger and adoration in his eyes it was as if she could feel the gaze as it brushed across the skin of her shoulders and her chest and then fell to her breasts. He dipped his head and gently ran his lips along the upper swells of each breast, not kissing but merely stroking the skin with his mouth so that his breath joined the evening air that swept across her nipples. Rain fought to control herself as desire for him flooded through her and settled in her core.

Lynx's mouth opened and his warm tongue glided over her breast and onto one tightened tip, encircling it and drawing it in so that he could suck it gently. His hand came up to cup the other, supporting its weight in his palm so that his finger and thumb could tease that nipple as his mouth did the other. Rain ran her hands up his thighs again, tightening slightly as they reached the juncture between his legs and his hips.

Finished with lavishing attention on her breasts, Lynx ran his hands up her sides so that he guided her arms up in the air beside her head. Rain held them in place as he took the gown that was bunched at her waist and led it up over her arms and off. He tossed it aside and she saw his eyes travel along her body luxuriously. With a soft moan of appreciation he reached forward and trailed his fingers down from the soft dip of her neck along her breastbone and onto her belly. She could feel her muscles shake and jump beneath his touch and her body tingled with growing need for him.

Keeping his eyes trained on her, Lynx peeled off his shirt

and tossed it over to join Rain's gown. She sighed at the sight of his beautifully chiseled body. She had grown accustomed to how much bigger he was than human men, but looking at his smooth skin and defined muscles still made her mouth water. As he brought his hand back to her belly, Rain lifted her eyes to look into his. She was still enraptured by the bright orange coloration of those wide orbs and she wondered if the color would ever lose its appeal for her. It wasn't just that it was so unusual for her, even though it was completely commonplace among the Denynso. Instead, the flicker of joy that came through her when she looked at them stemmed from knowing that he had not been born with eyes that color. Instead, it was finally completing his intended bond with her, his lifelong mate, which transformed his eyes to the color of the sunset. They were a visible signal to anyone who looked at him that he was bound to her and would be devoted to her throughout his entire existence.

Lynx rose to his knees to remove his pants and Rain couldn't resist reaching forward and wrapping her hand eagerly around the surging erection that was already pressing toward her. He drew in a sharp breath at the touch of her hand and she increased the pressure, slightly tightening her grip and running her hand down the length of him and then back up to the head so that she could gather the drops of slick fluid that were forming at the tip. She used them to help her hand slide quickly and smoothly along him, enjoying the feeling of his skin sliding across the hardened muscle beneath it. Lynx lifted his knees carefully and pushed his pants off, kicking them away without pulling away from her adoring touch.

His hand came to her cheek again and he stroked it softly, letting his thumb brush across her lips. Rain parted them slightly and touched the tip of her tongue to his skin. He slipped the pad into her mouth and she sucked on it gently. Lynx moaned low in his throat and Rain felt her stomach clench with the depth of her desire. He withdrew his thumb from her mouth and without needing any more of an invitation she leaned forward to replace it with the head of his erection. She sighed at the taste of him, allowing it to coat her tongue as she slipped her tongue into the slit and then ran it around the edge of the head, stopping to concentrate on the sensitive bundle of nerves on the underside.

She could heard Lynx groan at the attention she was giving him and after a moment she felt his hand tuck beneath her chin so that he could gently pull her away from him and guide her up onto her knees. When her body was touching his, she tilted her head to offer her mouth to him and he accepted it eagerly, drawing her closer as he kissed her so that his tongue explored the furthest reaches of her mouth and her breasts crushed against his chest. She felt one arm wrap around her waist firmly and guide her off of her knees and onto her back. Lynx came down over her, staring into her eyes as their bodies melded together.

Rain accepted him into her, drawing back her legs to open further so that he could sink in fully. He fit inside of her with such perfection it was as though he were part of her that always belonged there. She wrapped her legs around his hips, holding him as close within her and against her as she could. Lynx rested his forehead against hers and she saw his eyes close briefly before opening again to look into hers. He rolled his hips against her with incredibly control, nurturing her with long, slow strokes.

Bringing her hands to his back, Rain ran her fingers from his shoulder blades down to his hips, taking them in her hands so that she could pull him even deeper inside of her. The movement caused him to hit an achingly sensitive place within her and Rain cried out. The sound seemed to inspire Lynx and he thrust into her again, lifting up onto his knees to give himself even more leverage. Rain gasped with the intensity of the sensations that he was building within her and her body started to shake. Lynx continued, moving within her harder and faster until she felt her pleasure spiraling out of control and her walls closed tightly around him.

The squeeze of her body pushed Lynx over the edge and he buried his head down into the curve of her shoulder and neck so that her skin could muffle the scream of bliss pouring out of his chest. Rain could feel his cock throbbing within her and the thought of him spilling into her, filling her as he never had with anyone else pushed her even further, seeming to renew her orgasm so that her body milked his with each deep spasm.

Lynx remained buried deeply within her as they both came down from their earth shattering climaxes. When they had finally cooled enough that they could move, Rain reached beside her and pulled a blanket roll beneath her head while Lynx pulled another blanket up and over them. He was still nestled inside her body and she savored the feeling, not wanting it to end. Her eyes drifted closed and she fell asleep not to the sound of screams, but to the sound of Lynx's slow, even breath and deep, steady heartbeat.

5

———

They were walking before the sun touched the horizon the next morning. In the shady, purple-blue light of near dawn they walked as a loose cluster with the goal that since they knew where they were going this time, they would be able to make it to the settlement by nightfall that night rather than having to camp again and devote more of another day, leaving the captive Mikana in their state of unsureness for a moment longer than they truly had to.

Lynx felt at peace as they walked. He loved this time of day. He savored the softness of the air around him and the quiet of a world that had not quite yet woken. It was in these moments that a day always had potential and he felt like he could accomplish anything that he needed to.

"We didn't just leave immediately, you know."

Lynx turned toward Rain's voice as she suddenly spoke, breaking the silence among them.

"What?" he said.

"When we got to the prison planet, the one that they call

Penthos now. We didn't just leave as soon as we got there and noticed trouble. We stayed and fought."

"Rain, you don't have to talk about this," Lynx said, touching his mate's hand reassuringly.

"I know I don't," she said confidently, "but I feel like everyone, especially Ivy, deserves to know what really happened on that mission."

"Why especially me?" Ivy asked, sounding slightly taken aback by the assertion.

"You and the other humans are the only ones who even knew that we ever existed before the Denynso found us. They know what we've told them, but you've grown up going through school and being told all sorts of stories and legends about us. I think that you deserve to know the real story of what happened from someone who was actually there. Even though we say that when the others get back to Earth they can be discreet and stay anonymous, we all know that it is not going to stay that way for long. Eventually someone is going to figure out who they are and then chaos will ensue. The story is going to get even more complicated than it already is and there are going to be those people who villainize us and get angry because of the myths that other people created. I want to be able to tell you right from my own mouth everything that I remember about my time on the prison planet, my interaction with the Valdicians, and how we ended up on Uoria."

"Do you still remember everything after all this time?" Ivy asked.

"You have to remember," Rain said, "it has been far longer in your eyes than it has in mine. It has been only 15 years for me, and what I went through, 15 years is by far not long enough for me to forget. I don't even know if I would have forgotten if it had been more than 100."

"Are you sure?" Lynx asked quietly.

After seeing the look of horror and pain on her face the night before as she attempted to tell him what had happened, he didn't want her to feel like she had to go through all of that again. He had wanted to know more about what she went through so that he could feel like he knew her even better and that he could be there for her in the way that she deserved her mate to be, but he didn't want to put her through the turmoil of reliving those moments if he didn't absolutely have to.

"I am," she said, squeezing his hand as she turned to give him a small, reassuring smile. "Last night I started bringing forward memories that I hadn't let myself think about in a long time, and even though it was really difficult to think about them again and to face those demons and those questions, I feel like it was something that I needed to do. If I never talk about them, and I never tell anyone else so that they can know what actually happened, they will continue to eat at me forever and the same things or even worse could happen again because no one knows what to look for or what to do to prevent it."

"Things are different now," Ivy contended. "What happened to you wouldn't happen anymore."

"Every generation thinks that they know so much better than the ones that came before them and that they are going to be the ones that end all of the hardships and tragedies that exist in the universe. They think that they are the ones that would never do anything wrong or cause any pain to anyone. The problem is that they are always wrong. Death and suffering never change, and the curse of those who think that it does is that they rarely see what is happening. They think that everything is perfect until something horrible happens and then they are able to look back and condemn those who caused the pain, and even those who they think allowed the pain to happen. We will always be a step behind those who come after us. I am getting to see that in a way that you never will, but you have to trust me when I tell you that the generations that come after you are going to look back and wonder how you could possibly do things so wrong. All you can do is put all of your effort into doing as little wrong as you can and fixing as much of what happened before you as possible."

"I'm sorry," Ivy whispered, her head lowering to look at her feet as they crossed the open area of the planet rather than keeping eye contact with Rain.

"I know that I would be very interested in hearing more about what happened," Rey offered. "Now that we know that so much of the history of this planet and its species is inter-twined, I would like to know more about what happened. Especially considering what we know about our kind and its interactions with the Covra, it might help us understand everything more if we know how the first humans came to be here."

Lynx saw Maxim nod in agreement. Even as he nodded, though, Lynx noticed that the young Mikana man reached out to take Ivy's hand, offering his comfort and support to his partner. Though neither of them were Denynso, Lynx could see much the same attachment between those two as he did between mates of his kind. He knew that they didn't have the bonding ritual that the Denynso did, an experience that ensured that the members of his kind would only ever commit themselves to the person who they were intended to be with and that once the bond was complete they would never be apart, but they looked at each other with the same passion, intense connection, and total devotion that he did when he looked at Rain.

Rain looked at each of them and nodded as if making an agreement with them that she would continue her story. Adjusting her bag on her shoulder, she focused her eyes ahead in the direction they were walking and continued.

"As soon as we stepped off of the ship, we knew that the conditions on the planet were far worse than we ever could have imagined. The air smelled like smoke and blood, and there was never a moment of silence. All around us we could hear the screams of the prisoners and the shouts of the Valdicians who were holding them captive. We didn't know how many prisoners there were or what types of species they might be. We didn't even know how they had come to be on the planet. The intelligence that we had gotten only explained that they were prisoners of war, not prisoners of any type of crime, and that many were reported stolen from other planets without any concept of where they might have ended up. We knew that finding them and being able to release them,back to their own planets would help to prevent an intergalactic war that would have likely had devastating consequences that would still be reverberating through existence even now."

"You mentioned last night that there were walls around the buildings," Lynx said. "How did you get through them and into the colony?"

"Sheer force," Rain said. "The walls were massive, but they were poorly guarded considering the purpose of the colony. I suppose that the Validicians figured since they were the only ones that even knew that that planet existed and that there was little chance of anyone being able to find them by accident, they didn't really need the level of extensive security that most prison compounds have. We were able to approach the walls without even being noticed, and by the time that any of the Valdicians had realized that we were even there, more than half of those of us who had left the ship to go into the colony had already scaled the wall."

"How could they not notice a Star City ship landing on their planet? Wouldn't they have seen it orbiting and known it was landing?" Maxim asked.

"I really don't know," Rain said. "I would think that at least some of them did notice, but the Valdicians are single-minded, cruel, and conniving creatures. It is possible that those who noticed knew that they would have the upper hand against us and so rather than attacking immediately they took the time to tell others and prepare themselves. All I know is that when I landed on the ground on the other side of the wall, none of the Valdicians were anywhere near us. It wasn't until we had gotten close to the first building that they came after us."

"What did they look like?" Lynx asked.

All he could think about was Ty. Now that they knew that he came from a line that had Valdician blood, he wondered how many of the traits and characteristics he got from those creatures. He knew that the cruelty was not one of them, but Ty was brilliant and had inherited the stunning ability to move objects with his mind from a father he had lost far too soon.

"They were very tall, like the Denynso, but not as big. Their skin was pale to the point of almost being translucent, but their eyes and hair were like coal. As soon as they started toward us, we realized that we weren't contending with anything like what we had prepared for, and this mission was not going to be anywhere near as fast or seam-less as we had hoped. Rather than using weapons, the Valdicians simply picked members of the crew up and tossed them. The only way that we could fight back was to get behind them and attack with our own weapons. I knew that there was little that I could do in terms of fighting them off, but I was still determined to help any of the prisoners who I could, so I broke away from the battle and ran into the colony."

She stopped talking and Lynx looked at her. The struck, terrified look had returned to her face and he knew that she was reliving the horrors that she saw within that prison camp.

"What happened, Rain?" he asked, trying to gently guide her forward.

He truly didn't want to hear anymore, but he knew how important it was to her to tell her story and he wanted her to know that he was there beside her, protecting her.

"I found them," she said. Her voice had become dull and even, sounding almost as though the words weren't coming from her at all. "I have never seen anything like what I found in that compound and I hope with everything inside me that I never will. I expected to find the prisoners in cells, possibly chained within the buildings. Instead, many of them were chained along the outer walls of the buildings, suspended several inches off of the ground so that they had to either pull themselves up by their arms constantly or suffer the cutting of the cuffs into their wrists and the drag of their entire bodyweight on their shoulders. Some you could see had already dislocated their joints and were merely dangling from the chains. They had given up."

"What did you do?" Maxim asked.

"I knew that I didn't have much time, so I released the shackles of the ones that looked the healthiest and the most capable of fighting and getting out alive."

"Their chains weren't locked?"

Lynx saw Rain shake her head. The darkness in her eyes made it seem like she wasn't even there and he found himself praying that it wouldn't always be there, that she would come back from the memories.

"It was part of the Valdician's torture. They used shackles that connect with a latch rather than a key, but the latch was just out of reach so even though all the person in the shackles would have to do is flip the latch in the right direction, they weren't able to. They had to hang there knowing that they were just a few centimeters away from being able to get out, and staring at the others knowing that there was nothing that they could do for each other. I released a few of the prisoners and gave them the supplies and weapons that I had carried in. By this time the Valdicians had started back into the colony and were starting to fight against the prisoners I had freed. At some point one of them lifted me off of the ground with his thoughts and threw me against one of the buildings.

Everything after that moment is very disconnected. I remember opening my eyes and all I could see was flames and smoke. I don't even know what was burning, but the air was so thick I could barely breathe. When I did manage to get a breath in, it burned in my lungs. I couldn't stand, but I felt someone grabbing my arm and yanking me to my feet. Everything around me was fire, smoke, and screams as I ran. We barely made it out of the colony. It was like I could feel them at my heels and as I ran all I could think was that at any moment I was going to be in the air again and this time I wasn't going to survive the impact of my landing. But we made it to the ship and back inside. When I think back on it now I wonder if they were chasing us on purpose, not to catch us but to get to our ship. They could have incapacitated us at any moment, but instead they just chased after us until we got to the ship and inside. I could hear things hitting the sides of the ship as we tried to take off. Then I thought that the Valdicians were hitting it, but now I know that it was the weapons.

The weapons that they used were unlike anything that any of us had ever heard of. It wasn't until much later that we realized that they were throwing these tiny spheres at the ship. They latched on and turned into robotic creatures that were able to infiltrate the actual structure of the ship, bypassing the control system and setting into action a course programmed by the Valdicians."

"How long did it take you to realize that you weren't going back toward Earth?"

"It didn't take long. We weren't far from the planet when we realized that our commander was no longer in control of the ship. We tried to reach out to mission control, but all of our communication systems had been destroyed. I think that I knew then that nothing was ever going to be the same. I just didn't want to admit it to myself. For the rest of the journey the crew tried to figure out what was controlling the systems and override it, but they couldn't. By the time that we got close to Uoria, most of us were in survival mode. Obviously none of us knew where we were or what was happening, but we knew that if we were going to land, we were going to have to figure out how to get through it."

"Did you know that you were crashing?" Lynx asked.

"I felt the control of the ship leave. I don't know how to explain it any other way. I could feel it carrying us and then suddenly it just wasn't anymore. Not all of us had the chance to get into our seats before the crash. It seemed like it was only a few seconds, but I'm sure that it took longer. It just seemed like we were flying one moment and then the next we were plummeting and then the ship hit the ground. I've never heard anything sound that loud. The impact destroyed all of the systems inside so it was suddenly pitch black. Even the emergency lights wouldn't turn on.

I remember scrambling to take off my safety straps and trying to claw my way through the darkness to get out. I could hear the hissing of the electronic systems and the fuel tanks, and I knew that there was going to be an explosion. As I was climbing through the control room trying to find my way out I felt something grab my ankle and I kicked it away thinking that it was a piece of the controls. I wondered every day after that if it could have been one of the crew that we later found dead in the wreckage trying to get me to help him escape. When I was nearly at the exit, I felt my feet slip and I fell. I cut my arm, but later I found blood on the bottoms of my boots and I knew that's what made me slip.

When the explosion finally did come it was like the world was ending around me. I had managed to run far enough away from the ship that I wasn't seriously injured, but I knew that there were many of my crewmates, my friends, who had been in the recesses of the ship and there was no way that they would have been able to get out. I heard them screaming and it brought me back to the prison colony and the screams of the prisoners. It all became one sound in my mind.

I wish I could tell you that I remember everything that happened after we crashed, but the truth is that the first few days, maybe even weeks, are so blurred together I can't remember what really happened then. I know that despite what I really knew deep in my heart, I kept telling myself that someone would come for us. Even while we were sending out scouts to try to figure out somewhere we could place our camp. Even as we were going through the wreckage and pulling out the bodies so that we could bury them. Even as the sunrises and sunsets blended together and we realized that we needed shelter so we started breaking down what was left of the ship to build the settlement. I lived in a state of balanced torment. There were moments when I felt like I was going along with life on this new, strange planet absolutely fine and that we would all be OK, and then there were moments when I started thinking about it and I became desperate to find away off of the planet. I knew that someone had to be looking for us and that eventually they would find us, or that we would find a way to rebuild our ship and send at least a few people back to Earth for help.

Finally I let it all go. I realized that no matter how much I wanted to think that the people of Earth wouldn't simply let us disappear and never come find us, that that is exactly what happened and we were never going to leave. I was never going to see my parents again. I would never see my sister get married or have children. I would never again see all of the places that I loved. This empty, unknown planet was my home now, and gradually it started to look more beautiful. I was fortunate. I realized the truth and settled into living my life out on Uoria far earlier than some of the people. I don't think that it was until the first baby was born on the settlement that some people really got it through their minds that that was it. We were done. Earth and its people were only a memory and this was where the rest of our lives would play out."

6

"They didn't forget about you."

Maxim felt his mate's hand slip from his and watched as she stared at Rain, her face tense with an emotion he couldn't quite identify.

"What?" Rain asked, turning to look at Ivy.

"The people of Earth didn't forget about you. You said that you realized that they had just not bothered to look for you, that they didn't come to find you and that's why you had to stay here on Uoria. That isn't what happened."

Maxim could feel the tension rising between the two and he looked to Lynx, the appointed leader of the expedition, to gauge how he was reacting. He seemed calm, watching the interaction without saying anything.

"That's how I felt, Ivy."

"But that's not what happened. You act like you don't remember what Zuri told you. They named the entire planet after lamentation and mourning because of how deeply they felt about losing you. There was no way for them to know what happened to you. You didn't even know where you were, how did you expect for them to know how to find you? We've lived our entire lives hearing about the heroics of Project Nyx 23 and you are making it seem like you were just tossed aside."

"That's not what I meant. You have no idea what it's like to be on a completely unknown planet, have no idea why you are there, or what you are going to do, and then to have a species that you have never even heard of come after you and try to destroy you. That's what we went through. It would have been impossible for us not to think about mission control and the rest of the people on Earth and wonder why they didn't come for us. It might not have been logical, but it was what we went through. We looked up into the sky every night and knew that somewhere out there, among all of those stars, was our planet, and we wondered if we would ever see it again. We wondered if anyone out there had realized that we were gone and how long it would take for them to start looking for us. Eventually those thoughts and all of the hope that came with them faded."

"It wasn't their fault," Ivy said. "They did come for you."

"What did you learn about what happened to them and how the military responded?" Lynx asked.

"Mission control alerted the government as soon as they realized that they had lost communication with the ship. It was a clandestine mission so not everyone knew that it was even happening, but that also meant that it was especially dangerous. Any changes in protocol were taken very seriously. Less than 12 hours after mission control was not able to get in touch with you and was not getting a response, a team of special operative military units were sent to Penthos. That was when they told the rest of the people of Earth what was happening. Everyone was put on alert. There was some concern that the ship had been high jacked and that it would return but with the crew being held hostage. The government instructed the people of Earth to be prepared in case the ship landed in their area. Of course, it never did.

The military units got to the prison colony as quickly as they could, but you weren't there. We were taught that there was a massive conflict and the Valdicians were destroyed with Earth taking over the planet and declaring it uninhabitable."

"What happened to the prisoners who were still there when we left?" Rain asked. Her voice sounded slightly desperate and her eyes were wide as she searched Ivy's face for any detail. "I know some of them had to have survived. Some of them had to have made it out of the colony and survived on the outskirts of the planet long enough for the military units to arrive and rescue them."

"We were told that the military units liberated them and sent them back to their original planets."

"Sent them back?" Maxim asked.

"The military operative traveled in several different ships so that they could arrange a more complex attack. After destroying the Valdicians, one of the ships was rerouted as a rescue ship to bring the freed prisoners home."

"Did you ever find out who those prisoners were? What kind of species or what planets they came from? Anything?" Rain asked.

Ivy shook her head.

"No. The military never released that information. They said that they didn't want to cause any more pain to those who had suffered by rehashing what had happened to them."

"What did they do to the planet? To Penthos?"

"What do you mean?"

"After they named it, what did they do with the planet?

Is there a memorial there or anything? Has anyone gone back there since the military units left?"

"Not that I know of," Ivy said. "The government announced that it had declared the planet uninhabitable and off-limits to everyone within the galactic federation. There are memorials on Earth, but as far as I know no one is allowed to travel there."

Maxim thought over what Ivy had told them. Something about the stories that Rain and Ivy had told didn't make sense to him, but he couldn't quite figure out what it was.

"No one ever found out who sent the intelligence about the prison colony?" he asked.

"No," Rain responded. "It was anonymous. One of the members of our organization brought it to our commander, but wasn't able to tell us where she got it."

Maxim made a soft sound of acknowledgement.

"What is it, Maxim?" Ivy asked.

"I'm not sure," he said. "It just all seems so strange to me. If the Valdicians really were as ruthless as Rain says that they are, who could have possibly found out about the prison colony and sent the information to Earth without getting caught? And how could they have suddenly made the decision to send you to Uoria? Did they just happen to have the technology to override your ship's operating systems and disable the communication devices sitting around at such easy reach that they were able to grab it in the midst of a battle?"

"What are you saying?" Rain asked.

"I don't know," Maxim responded. "It just doesn't make sense. They would only have developed that technology if they intended to use it. Could it really be a coincidence that when you arrived they just decided to use it and it perfectly led to them sending you to their allies?"

"We were lured there," Rain said.

Maxim could feel the startled emotions coming off of Rain as she started to piece together what he was telling her.

"What do you mean 'lured'?" Lynx asked.

"Whoever sent the intelligence that the Valdicians had an illegal prison colony on that planet knew about our department. They were trusting the fact that when we heard about the colony we would send a team to investigate," Rain said. "They wanted us to come. They weren't surprised by us. They were expecting us. This wasn't an accident. Us getting stranded here wasn't some convenient event for the Valdicians. They planned it. They wanted to send us to the Covra. They didn't realize that our voices would be their greatest weakness."

Rain sounded angry now, as if emotions that she had long suppressed were starting to come out of her.

"Maxim," Rey said, stopping him before he was able to respond to Rain.

Maxim looked up and saw the outline of the settlement wall against the horizon in front of them. His feet stopped moving as if by their own volition and he felt his breath pause in his lungs for a moment. They had finally made it. They were only a matter of steps away from the arched entryway that would lead him back to his people, to his brother who was suffering in the captivity of the meeting hall, not knowing what had happened to Maxim or if he would ever return. For now, questions about the Valdicians and who had brought Nyx 23 to the prison planet would have to wait.

Without saying another word, Maxim pushed forward. Everything around him seemed to fade as his steps quickened until he was running toward the settlement, no longer feeling the weight of the packs on his back or slung over his shoulders. He could hear the pounding of the footsteps of the rest of the group running to catch up with him, but he didn't stop. When he finally reached the arched entryway built into the worn, weathered stone wall surrounding the settlement he paused and glanced back over his shoulder. Just as he was turning back around he felt a hand clamp down on his other shoulder.

"So you've come back," a voice growled.

Maxim looked up to see Vax, the Denynso who had so vehemently agreed with Pyra's intention to destroy the entire Mikana clan, standing only inches from him, his massive hand gripping Maxim's shoulder painfully. Rather than feeling intimidated, Maxim was angry. He shrugged out of Vax's grip and squared his chest to him. Though his size was no match for the warrior, he refused to back down.

"I'm here to release my clan," he said calmly and evenly.

Vax laughed, his hand moving to his hip and the hilt of the knife that Maxim could see tucked into a sheath at his waistband. The move was subtle, but threatening, and Maxim felt his muscles tense in response.

"You will do nothing of the kind," Vax said through gritted teeth. "We are under the command of Pyra to keep the filthy creatures quarantined in the meeting hall."

"And we are under command of Creia to have you release them."

Maxim turned when he heard Lynx's voice behind him. In his intense standoff with Vax he hadn't noticed that the others had caught up with him. Now Lynx was holding the letter that Creia had given him before they left and staring down Vax. There was seething tension between the two warriors as they both stared at each other with expressions that said they still felt the other was wrong and a betrayal to his kind.

"What did you say?" Vax asked.

"Creia has sent us to release the Mikana and welcome them back to our compound if they want to come. If not, they are free to return to their kingdom. The warriors are to report back to the compound as soon as possible to perform guard rounds while the others are on Earth."

"They still went?" Vax asked, sounding both shocked and infuriated.

"Yes. Now bring us to the meeting hall."

"Let me see that letter."

Lynx handed the letter over to Vax, who glared down at it. His strong hand gripped the edge of the parchment so hard Maxim worried that it would tear it before they were able to get it to the warriors standing guard outside of the meeting hall. After a few seconds of examining the letter, Vax shoved it back at Lynx and made a huffing sound. It was obvious that he hated the situation that he was now in, but as a Denynso warrior his first loyalty was to the king and he was not able to deny him. No matter what he thought of the Mikana, he was at the mercy of the monarch's command and had to help the appointed group release the captives and then return to the compound.

Vax stepped out of the way and the group entered the settlement, stepping into the aftermath of Pyra's reign.

7

———

The streets of the settlement were unnervingly quiet. If he hadn't known that they were there, Maxim would have thought that none of the humans had remained when they left the settlement. They followed behind Vax and Maxim looked around intently, trying to find any hint of the people who lived there, of life continuing on after they started for the Denynso compound.

"Where is everyone?" Rain finally asked from behind him.

"They are in their homes," Vax said sternly.

"All of them?" Rain asked. "Why?"

"They have finished their services for the day and are at home where they belong."

"Where they belong?" Rain snapped, pushing past Maxim so that she was walking closer to Vax. "Where they belong according to who?"

"Pyra," Vax said simply. "You were here. You know the schedule that he created for the people of this settlement when they came under his command. They perform their services during the day and they spend the rest of their time in their homes. By controlling them, we keep them safe."

"Safe from who?" Maxim asked, the anger starting to build inside him. "The only ones who these people need to be kept safe from is you."

"They aren't under Pyra's command anymore," Rain said. "You have no right to keep them locked in their homes. They spent enough time stuck where someone else told them to stay. That's over now."

"I promised my allegiance and obedience to Pyra. This is what he wanted."

The words made Maxim's stomach feel sick. The blind, unwavering level of devotion and following of the lead warrior was disturbing.

"Pyra isn't here," Rain said, "and he isn't in command of anyone any longer."

"Creia disagreed with Pyra," Lynx said. "He told him that what he did here was wrong and that he had failed all of us. If you continue to insist that you will follow Pyra's commands, you are going against your king, your people, and even Pyra himself. He has denounced his actions and expressed deep regret for what he did while he was here."

Maxim could see a vein in Vax's neck throb and his jaw tighten even further. He didn't say another word to them, but as he approached the meeting hall Maxim saw him step up to one of the guards.

"Tell the people of the settlement that they are no longer under our control and that they may leave their homes and go about their lives as they wish."

The words carried hopeful sentiment, but the sound of his voice was still gruff. Maxim knew that regardless of how Creia, and even Pyra, felt, Vax was still firmly in the belief that the Mikana were not worth allowing to live. He could not be trusted, and Maxim was looking forward to the slightly older warrior leaving to return to the compound.

The other warrior looked at Vax strangely and then evaluated the group that had followed him. He met eyes with Lynx and Lynx stepped forward to show him the letter from Creia. After reading it, the warrior handed the parchment back to him and started down the main street, stopping at homes as he went to pound on the doors. Vax started around to the back of the building and as they followed him Maxim could hear the other warrior relaying the same message to the people who were streaming out of their homes that Vax had given him.

When they reached the back of the meeting hall they found two warriors flanking the door. They had a slightly worn look as if the days of standing guard on a continuously rotating schedule that offered precious little time to sit and even less to sleep was starting to drag on them. Lynx started to step forward and then came back and turned around to face Rey.

"I think that it is your place to do this," he said respectfully, offering the parchment from Creia to the leader of the Mikana kingdom.

Rey looked at him for a bit and then took the parchment from his hand slowly. Maxim could see the light in his leader's eyes, the light that had slowly disappeared while they were in the settlement and had gone completely the morning that Maxim discovered the changing of his skin, start to return. Rey stepped up to the warriors, both of whom turned their heads only slightly and glared at him.

"I come with a proclamation from your king releasing the Mikana from your control and your guard. They are to be let out of the meeting hall immediately and permitted to do as they wish."

One of the warriors took the parchment from Rey's hand and examined it before handing it off to the other, who also read it. He handed the parchment back to Rey who gave it to Lynx and then looked into the eyes of each of the warrior guards in turn.

"Now, men," he said, his voice sounding firmer and more confident than Maxim had heard it in a long time.

The warriors stepped away from the building and one of them released the large, heavy latch that kept the door in place. There was a rush of sound as soon as the door swung open and for a moment Maxim thought that it was the sound of air moving through the tight hallway, but then realized that it was voices from deep inside the building. Rey stepped inside and Maxim came up behind him, wanting to get in to the others as quickly as possible.

They had only taken a few steps down the close, stale-smelling hall when Danye, one of the young members of the kingdom, stepped out of one of the rooms that led off of the hall and faced them. He was holding a small bowl in his hands but he dropped it as soon as he saw Rey and Maxim. A smile broke across a face that looked weathered despite being trapped inside a room for days, and aged well beyond his years.

"Rey?" he said, sounding unsure of himself as if he thought that he was conjuring up the image of his leader and friend. "Maxim?"

Rey stepped forward and gathered Danye in an embrace, patting him on the back. When the hug ended, Danye turned down the hallway and shouted to the others.

"Rey and Maxim are back!" he yelled. He seemed to

suddenly notice the flow of evening light coming into the hallway from the open door and his smile only widened. "The door is open! The guards are gone!"

The hallway filled with the members of the Mikana kingdom. Their voices blended and lifted in the tight space, surrounding Maxim until he felt nearly overwhelmed by them. He made his way through the men gathering in the hall, pushing through in search of his brother. Finally he emerged from the hall into the room where they had been gathered when Pyra brought the decision down that they would be quarantined there until a final decision was made about their fate. Just stepping into the space brought back the panicked memories of standing there helplessly, watching as Loralia created a wall without windows or doors that cut the meeting room in half and blocked them in that small portion of the building.

"Maxim!"

Kyven's voice cut through the din created by all of the others and Maxim felt his heart lift. By the time he turned toward the sound, his brother was gathering him into his arms. Maxim held Kyven to himself tightly, gripping his shirt and rocking him slightly.

"Are you alright?" he asked, pushing back and looking at his younger brother's face carefully.

"Yes," Kyven answered.

"Are you sure?"

"Yes. I knew you'd come back for me."

Maxim felt a sudden pang of guilt. Escaping from the meeting hall with Ivy and running away from the settlement had been one of the most difficult decisions that he had ever made. He had left his brother behind, not knowing if he was ever going to see him again, not knowing if Kyven was even going to survive the ordeal. Maxim was glad he had done what he did, though. Had he not listened to Ivy and gone with her when she had come for him, they wouldn't have encountered Pyra in the wreckage and forced him along with the others to agree that what happened to the Mikana wasn't his decision to make.

"I didn't abandon you," Maxim said, holding his brother's face in both hands and looking at him in the eyes. "You know that, don't you?"

"I know, Maxim."

The sound of the voices in the hallway was lessening and Maxim realized the men were finally leaving the building. He started toward the hallway, but felt Ivy pull him back.

"I need you to stay in here with me for just a minute with no one else," she said.

Maxim looked at Kyven and held up a finger.

"Just one minute," he said. "Go outside. Breathe some fresh air. I will be right out."

Kyven nodded and hurried toward the door. Even though he was only slightly less than a year younger than Maxim was, Kyven suddenly seemed so young and vulnerable. When the voices all dissipated and the room fell silent, Maxim let Ivy pull him toward her.

"What is it?" he asked.

"There's something we need to do," she said.

Releasing his hand, she stepped up toward the wall that Loralia had created. It had been the most astonishing thing that Maxim had ever seen, and even now he didn't understand how she had done it, or how Ivy had managed to bypass it to bring him out onto the other side with her. He saw her lift her hands and rest them for a moment on the surface of the wall, her shoulders falling with a sigh.

"What are we doing?" he asked.

"Come here."

Maxim walked up to her and Ivy turned away from the wall to take both of his hands in hers.

"Do you believe that I'm here?" she asked.

"Of course I do," he said, leaning forward to touch his forehead to hers.

"Even if someone told you that I wasn't, would you still believe it?"

"Of course I would."

"Kiss me," she said.

As their lips touched Maxim could feel her take him by the arms and start to lead him away from the wall, guiding him along and up the steps of the well in the center of the floor until they were halfway up. She pulled away from him and looked at the wall.

"What are you doing, Ivy?"

"Do you believe that you can keep me safe? That you would never let anything happen to me?"

"I would never let anything hurt you?"

"Do you really believe that? Completely?"

"Yes. Ivy, what are you talking about?"

She was starting to scare him, and the fear only increased when she released his arms and started running down the steps toward the wall. She picked up speed as she went, but just before she would have crashed into it, she seemed to pass right through the wall. An instant later, he was looking at her on the other side of the room, the wall now gone. She smiled at him slightly breathlessly and they ran towards each other, meeting in an embrace on the platform in the center of the room.

"It was just a reflection," she said to him. "It was only real when you thought it was, but if we believed that it wasn't, it wasn't. You believed that no matter what, if you were with me, I was going to be safe, which means that I wouldn't hit that wall."

"What did you believe?"

"That when I turned around, you would be there."

TBC

(To be continued in book IV...)

www.ingramcontent.com/pod-product-compliance
Lightning Source LLC
Chambersburg PA
CBHW032044180726
48284CB00008B/2750